The Berenstain Bears'
THANKSGIVING

Library of Congress Cataloging-in-Publication Data

Berenstain, Stan.
    Berenstain Bears' Thanksgiving / Stan & Jan Berenstain.
        p.   cm.
    "Cartwheel books."
    Summary: Papa Bear thinks that Thanksgiving is the best holiday of all, but his
overreaction to the cubs' report of seeing Bigpaw in the woods teaches him an
important lesson about the meaning of the day.
    ISBN 0-590-94731-1
    [1. Bears — Fiction.   2. Thanksgiving Day — Fiction.   3. Prejudices — Fiction.
4. Stories in rhyme.]   I. Berenstain, Jan.   II. Title.
PZ8.3.B4493Bh jc   1997
[E] — dc20   96-38775
                                                                              CIP
                                                                               AC

12 11 10 9 8 7 6 5 4   9/9 0 1 2/0

                            Printed in the U.S.A.   37

                    First Scholastic printing, October 1997

The Berenstain Bears'
THANKSGIVING

Stan & Jan Berenstain

SCHOLASTIC INC.
New York Toronto London Auckland Sydney

It's 'round the next bend,
down a sunny dirt road.
Just ask the next squirrel,
caterpillar, or toad

for the tree-house home
of the Bear family,
where Ma, Pa, and the cubs
are cozy and warm
in their split-level tree.

Just at the moment,
inside their quaint home,
they're reading
the harvest honeycomb.

"Honeycomb dribble,
honeycomb drip,
what lies ahead?
A handsome stranger?
Money? A trip?

Grizzly growl,
grizzly grum,
warn us of any
danger to come!"

Then, Mama blew hard.
Loose flour flew.
Who caught the flour?
Papa, that's who.

But Mama and Papa
both had turned white—
Pa from the flour,
Mama from fright.

The sign in the pan,
stuck to the honey,
was no handsome stranger,
no trip, no money,

but a bone-chilling warning
of danger ahead,
the frightening footprint
of a great giant's tread.

"Bigpaw!" breathed Mama.
"Good grief and alas!
The Thanksgiving Legend
is coming to pass!"

"Legend?" asked Sister.
"What legend is that?"

"It says
when the Bears
of Bear Country
grow greedy and fat,
and fail to share
Nature's great bounty,
that monster of monsters,
Bigpaw, will come
and gobble up Bear Country
county by county!"

"Nonsense!" mocked Papa.
"Nonsense and stuff!
Nonsensical piffle!
Pure Bear Country guff!"

PRIVATE

But Papa Bear couldn't
have been more wrong.
The Thanksgiving Legend
was coming on strong.

Not more than ten
or twelve miles away,
at that very moment
of that very day,
in a dark, murky forest,
the ground was shaking.
From crane fly to croc,
swamp creatures
were quaking.

Something was coming.
The creatures were frantic.
Something enormous.
Something gigantic.

It was Bigpaw,
of course.
He was bigger by far
than Paul Bunyan's horse,

with shoulders like boulders,
ditto his knees,
with paws big as dumpsters
and arms thick as trees.

Out of the forest
he came and he went,

each footfall leaving
a monster-sized dent.

But Papa just scoffed
and puffed out his chest.
"Just forget about monsters
and all of the rest.
Because, my dears,
I beg to suggest,
when it comes to holidays,
your Papa knows best.

I'm a bear for holidays!
I like 'em all—

whether in winter,   spring,

summer,   or fall!

"And your Pa has perfect
holiday habits.
On Easter, I always
make way for rabbits,

and say a small poem
for spring and rebirth.

On Earth Day, of course,
I cherish the Earth.

"On Christmas Day,
I think of others—
fathers, mothers,
sisters, brothers.

On Arbor Day,
I talk to the trees.

But Thanksgiving's the best
holiday, if you please—
the one that for me
is really the winner.
Why?
Thanksgiving dinner!"

Yes, it was almost time
for the Bears' Thanksgiving,
the day they gave thanks
for their standard of living.

And what a standard it was!
From hollow to hill,
from glenloch to glade,
the bears of Bear Country
had it made!

Except for the legend!
The legend that said:
if the bears of Bear Country
were selfish and greedy

and insufficiently
kind to the needy,
giving them no more
than a tail or a wing,

then Bigpaw would come
AND DO HIS THING!

So as you can see
in Papa Bear's case,
all Thanksgiving meant
was feeding his face.

So they went to a place
that only they knew—
the mixed-nut forest
where the mixed-nut trees grew.

As the cubs picked almonds
and walnuts, pistachios, too,
which Papa Bear claimed
as his Thanksgiving due,
the entire forest
started to lurch.

The cubs fell like stones
from their top-lofty perch.

But they landed not
with a bone-jarring bump.
They landed instead
with a comfortable "whump."

For you see, the cubs
had been caught in mid-air
in the dumpster-sized paw
of a monster-sized bear.

It was Bigpaw, of course.
The monster HAD come.
Talk about scared!
The normally talkative
cubs were struck dumb.

Suffice it to say,
something surprising
happened that day.

With a bit of a smile
and nary a sound,
he gently placed them
down on the ground.

What a shock!
What a surprise!
For despite his
manner
and imposing size,
Bigpaw was nice,
gentle, and shy—
a friendly, helpful
sort of a guy.

Those cubs knew
what they had to do—
tell that only *part*
of the legend was true.

Though he was powerful,
fearsome, and tall,
the monster called Bigpaw
was no monster at all.

It was important news,
so off they hurried,
leaving Bigpaw looking
a little worried.

"Little cubs! Little cubs!
You forgot your mixed nuts!"
This certainly was true,
no *ifs*, *ands*, or *buts*.

When the cubs told Papa
their Bigpaw tale,
his eyes opened wide,
his face grew pale.

Pa didn't hear
the positive part.
All he heard was "Bigpaw."
The name struck terror
in Papa Bear's heart.

"Just hold on," said Mama.
"Whether or not the legend is true,
we must welcome the stranger.
It's the right thing to do."

But ignoring the news
that Bigpaw was nice
and paying no heed
to Mama's advice,
Papa Bear called up
the Bear National Guard.
They would deal with the stranger.
They would deal with him hard.

BEAR COUNTRY
WANTS YOU!

YAWN

Meanwhile Bigpaw had climbed
to a high mountain ledge.
He stretched and he yawned
as he looked over the edge.

As Bigpaw's yawns
rolled into the valley
through a mountain pass
known as Echo Alley,
they grew from a rumble
to an enormous roar,
and confirmed the bears' fears
about the Thanksgiving monster
of legend and lore.

Alas, Mama's protest
fell on deaf ears,
the bears of Bear Country
gave in to their fears.

Mama's advice
notwithstanding,
they put the cart of fear
before the horse
of understanding.

"To arms!" cried Papa.
"There's no time to fuss.
We've got to get him
before he gets us."

Swords were unsheathed.
Bugles were blown.
They were no longer bears
with minds of their own.

They were no longer
Jack and Jill, Betty and Bob.
The bears had become
a dangerous mob.

With the false courage of numbers
to the mountain they went,
with an arsenal of weapons
and deadly intent.

While up on the mountain
the cause of the flap
was settling down
for a bit of a nap
when he heard a strange sound.
It was still far away
and not very loud.
Of course, what it was
was the roar of a crowd.

Now Bigpaw was certainly
no mental wizard.
But he was getting a feeling
down deep in his gizzard
that trouble was coming.
So he scratched his head

and started his fuzzy
old noodle a-humming.
And using his powerful
arms and shoulders,
he built a tower,
a tower of boulders.

If those bears were to charge up
out of the valley,
they'd be just like pins
in a bowling alley.

But those bears kept on coming,
faster and faster!
There was simply no way
to avoid disaster!

But then—
at the very last instant
before the rocks fell—
there came through the din
a cub's high-pitched yell.

WAIT!

It was Sister.

"Wait!" Sister cried.
The rock tower teetered.
It started to slide.

Brother and Sister,
small and defiant,
had positioned themselves
in defense of the giant.

But Brother and Sister
were in terrible danger,
and there was no one
to help them . . .
EXCEPT FOR THE GIANT.

With the bears looking on
in amazement and shock,
Bigpaw held back
that tower of rock.
And with the great strength
of his mighty right arm,
he protected small Brother
and Sister from harm.

Bigpaw's our friend.
He's very nice.
He saved us once.
Now he's rescued us twice.

Weapons and hats
filled the air,
plus thankful shouts
from every bear.

There was joy in the valley
on that fateful day.
The bears welcomed the stranger;
yes, they had a debt to repay.

But it was more than that.
At Thanksgiving dinner
the very next day,
host Papa Bear
had this to say:
"Friends, we are thankful that
we've learned to share
our bounty with our fellow bear."

HOME
SWEET
TREE

Yes, friends, it was quite a Thanksgiving—
no *ifs*, *ands*, or *buts*!

• ABOUT THE AUTHORS •

Stan and Jan Berenstain have been writing and illustrating books about bears for more than thirty years. In 1962, their self-proclaimed "mom and pop operation" began producing one of the most popular children's book series of all time — **The Berenstain Bears**. Since then, children the world over have followed Mama Bear, Papa Bear, Sister Bear, and Brother Bear on over 100 adventures through books, cassettes, and animated television specials.

Stan and Jan Berenstain live in Bucks County, Pennsylvania. They have two sons, Michael and Leo, and four grandchildren.